The B

S.C. Towers

Disclaimer

The Beverly

Copyright © S.C. Towers 2023

The right of S.C. Towers to be identified as the author of this work has been asserted following the Copyright, Designs and Patents Act.

All rights reserved. No part of this publication may be reproduced, transmitted, or stored in a retrieval system in any form or by any means without the permission in writing from the copyright owner, nor otherwise circulated in any form of binding or cover other than that in which it is published and without a similar condition being imposed on the subsequent purchaser.

This is a work of fiction. All characters in this publication are fictitious, and any resemblance to real people, alive or dead, is purely coincidental.

Acknowledgements

Thanks must go to all my wonderful friends and family for being generally amazing and always supporting my writing.

Thank you, Clair, for your notes and invaluable input.

Joe, thank you for making me laugh every day.

Also, thanks to E and N, my two best little buddies and my inspiration, always.

S.C. Towers is from a small town in North-Northumberland where she lives with her husband and two daughters. As well as being a mother, she has worked in tourism and education, appeared on stage in various guises and has a degree in English Literature and Theatre from York St John University.
The Beverly is her first published novella.

For Dado

Contents

Episode One

The Sisters..1

Meghan..3

The Beverly...5

Damián..9

The Wife...12

Infamous...15

Episode Two

The Sister...23

The Letter...32

Memories...35

The Saviour..38

Episode Three

Unhappy Families...47

Truths and Lies..50

Fake News..54

The Eye of the Storm.......................................57

Episode Four

Lost..63

Home is Where the Hate Is....................................67

A Point of No Return..70

Hearts and Minds...72

The Bond that Binds Us...74

Episode Five

The Rough with the Smooth..................................83

A Present from the Past..86

Family Ties..90

Episode Six

The Phone-call..95

The Mother...98

The Reunion..100

Game Over..104

Together Again, Naturally....................................108

How Sweet it is..114

EPISODE ONE

The Sisters

The apartment was stuffy, the kind of stuffy you get when the man you love tells you he is leaving you for your sister. A lot to take in, granted, but surprisingly unsurprising. Jinger was not the kind of girl to get into anything heavy. She had known from the get-go that Preston was a player, but like a good Christian, she had ignored it and played along. So long as he came home to her bed every night, her heart let him in. Even Jocelyn was no mystery to her. Her sister had caught a net-full of good looks and charm, enough to win over any socialite in a game of chance. But trust had always been in their relationship. Trust and a handful of resentment. Jinger was the clever one, smart and savvy in a way that befits one who had to fend for herself, her sister not so. Trouble followed her like a shifting shadow, if it were not for Jinge all these years Joce would have been put away for good a long time ago.

She shuffled noiselessly towards the apartment door, her head banging with the trauma. Preston's face was glued to hers as though waiting for her reaction, expecting an explosion. It did not come. Jinger's face rapidly changed from confusion to a sense of understanding.

"You knew this day would come, didn't you hun? I mean, it's been on the cards for a while." Preston wanted to lunge forward and take her in his arms. She looked straight at him, caught for a moment a glimpse of something real, something heartfelt, then it melted away and she realised for the first time in their five-year relationship that none of it had been real.

"I have to leave now." she muttered, pulling her handbag off the floor, and reaching for the door handle.

"We can talk more later, if you want to." Preston was clinging on to the nothingness.

"Later. Yeah." Jinger opened the door and took a deep breath, it felt like freedom.

Meghan

Meghan Brock could be described as many things, but not compulsive. In terms of work, she was resourceful, economical and user friendly. Her approach was above reproach. Yet she had always felt as though something was missing. Her time in Rwanda had taught her to live life to the full and not to hold back on anything. She had met Trey as a teenager; a chance meeting in the last year of high school had given destiny a run for his money. So far, their lives had taken no misses and Trey had certainly had a few hits, his TV career allowing them luxuries considered excessive by her conservative stepfather. Meghan was a trained Physiotherapist but after too many handsy clients, she had taken on a less physical role at the only luxury Hotel for miles - The Beverly. Trey had seemed less than impressed with his partner's choice of career-change but had supported her need for something else, something without pressure. His own pressure, a weight carried by them both. His job took him to locations which allowed him some respite from his relationship. He classed it as an escape, not adultery. He was famous. It was justified. Meghan continued to miss him when he was away and counted down the days on her kitchen calendar until his return when they would love each other again.

It had been six years.

And yet on Saturday he left her. He could not give a reason, he just left. Shut the door calmly on his way out. Pulled out of the driveway as if it were an everyday occurrence. Meghan had continued with her day almost episodically, moving from one inane task to the next. Sunday came and went in a slow succession of red wine bottles. She strolled casually into work on Monday, sat at her desk and picked up the phone. It was only then that her heart broke.

The Beverly

As buildings go, the hotel had a quaintness to it. It was imposing, granted, yet still retained a pleasant charm and elegance like an ageing duchess settling down to high tea. Some said it was a modern building, disguised as a relic, but those who worked there knew its guise and kept its secrets.

For The Beverly held those secrets close and its inner workings even closer. To work there was to be part of something far bigger than anything that existed beyond its walls.

Those walls reached so high that you had to squint to see the upper levels. And often, if the sun were in the right place, you couldn't see them at all. That was how The Beverly liked it. White-washed walls, thick paned windows, clean and fresh as if brand new. If you stayed there, you felt clean, as though every worry you ever had disappeared when you stepped through those magnificent doors. It was the air inside too. It was intoxicating, exotic, and generous. You breathed it in, deep into your lungs, and believed in a new life. That was how The Beverly liked it.

Every inch was spotless. Every wall gleamed. No dark corners here. Only light was allowed. Imagine now a light that did not demand your eyes to adjust to it. Did not bear down on you. Did not thrum into your head. It feels warm. It welcomes your senses. It eases your mind. That was how The Beverly liked it.

****

Mitchell had purchased the business from an overly entitled rich kid. The guy's father had bequeathed it to him in his will, and like all spoiled brats, he just wanted the money. For years, Mitchell had worked in commercial management. The change was overdue. He had adopted an ornately decorated, high-ceilinged room as his office and made sure to add his own touches of sophistication to the embellished wall hangings. He collected modern-art. He couldn't admit to understanding any of it, but he thought it looked impressive; this only added weight to his particularly light gravitas. His wife, on the other hand, preferred bare walls and shelves; in this they were opposites.

Dellah Hudson nee Ramsey was Mitchell's wife. A petite, mid-thirties ex journalist, who after the birth of their son, had taken to being a housewife. Of course, with this new investment of his, she could have her own housewife. She refused, preferring to 'take care of her own.' His age had never been an issue to Dellah; she called it 'experience' and liked the security it gave her. His grey hairs were a sign of a life lived. To her, that meant safety and understanding and a competent father for Randy.

Mitchell kept a candid photo of his little family on the desk in his new office as a reminder of what could be so easily lost to him. His first (and only) relationship before Dellah had been agony. Melissa had certainly been no saint and yet he had loved her passionately. Their liaison had been a brief one. He knew she had a past, and he accepted her without questioning it. He even stood up for her in court when the charges were laid against her, and he still rallied for her cause when 'life' was decreed. Sometimes he thought of her, what might have been and then saw Dellah and Randy, their faces smiling as one and his thoughts turned from her. She had been dead for over twenty years. Suicide they said. He was still in therapy. Mitchell walked to the door of his new office and stepped out into the hotel lobby.

"Good morning, Mr Hudson," uttered the concierge.

"Good morning, Damián."

Damián

Damián smiled. He thought it was only polite to smile at his boss. This was his seventh year at the Beverly Hotel and already he had seen four new managers pass through. He liked this one. There was something normal about him, there was nothing hidden. Damián looked down at the monitor on his desk. On it he could see images of various areas of the hotel. The kitchen staff busily prepared room service, entrees and those exquisite Mediterranean octopus dishes the hotel had become famous for. Not many guests ate in the Michelin star restaurant. But when they did, it was a remarkable sight. In another corner of the screen, a maid was carefully wiping down one of the bathrooms, meticulously polishing the taps until they shone blindingly. He nodded in appreciation. On the other side of the hotel, the rubbish was being collected, tidily and quickly. No-one would want to witness that. Absolutely nothing went unseen by Damián.

And then, he saw her. The woman. She was standing in the lift. She had moved in with her partner over a month ago. The Beverly was not a place you stayed in for just a typical week. It was an exclusive hotel for those who had more money than anything else, for people who thought of money, as common people thought of tap-water. Most of them did not have careers and so spent their days on the beach or in the hotel Spa. Damián lived close by and took as many shifts as they offered him. Especially since the woman turned up. She was heading downstairs. The black and white image was distorted but he knew it was her. Her hair was thrown up into a bun; strands fell over her face. She looked up directly into the camera and he caught a glisten in her eyes. She was tapping her foot erratically, she seemed tense. The lift door opened, and she stepped out. She made her way to the desk and Damián made sure not to look up straight away. He could smell her warm perfume coming towards him.

"I'm just letting you know that I won't be coming back Damián," she said, leaning purposefully against the desk.

"I'm sorry to hear that, Miss Landley." he replied, moving his eyes towards hers and catching a redness around the sockets.

"Mr Hargreaves will be flying solo from now on."

"I do hope we shall see you again, Miss Landley?" he went on to enquire, as if reading from a script.

"I doubt that very much, Damián, but thank you for everything." The woman pushed herself away and shoved her hands into her jeans' pockets. She strode towards the exit and smiled one last smile at him. Then, she was gone. Her perfume still lingered around the desk. He breathed it in carefully, and then sat down again and looked at the screen. He could feel a prickling sensation rise on his neck and begin to travel down his spine. He had lost her. This game was over. Now he needed to play a new hand.

"Good morning Damián. Have you seen my husband about?" asked a voice.

The Wife

Dellah was a regular at the hotel. Her presence was important to Mitchell, and it got her out of the house. She also liked to keep an eye on him. All these rich women in their expensive clothes brought out the jealous side in Dellah Hudson. She knew she was his confidant, but Mitchell kept his past remarkably close to his chest. He was not keen on detail. They had first met in a bar the night Dellah had discovered her father in bed with her best friend. Mitchell had held her so close that night and still had not really let go since. She liked the feelings he gave her; she felt safe even when he was not around. Which was a lot lately. Their eight years of marriage had produced only one child, a now boisterous five-year-old with his father's curls and his mother's dark eyes. He had just started school and Dellah found herself worrying constantly. Randy was named after Mitchell's father, a man who had single handedly brought up six children after his wife was murdered in a supermarket robbery.

The concierge, Damián, had been here when Mitchell bought the place. She had held back until now, not wanting to get too close to a man who belonged to her own past. He would not remember her; he had known her by another name - the once young, vivacious *'Christine'*. She had looked into his grey eyes, and she had seen Hell.

****

"Where's Meghan this morning?" she asked Damián, carefully.

He looked up from the screen and smiled. Dellah could not match his gaze.

"She said she'd be delayed this morning ma'am." His lips a smooth line, eyes unblinking.

She smiled back then sighed, catching his full attention.

"Can I help you with anything, Mrs Hudson?" Always quick to respond, Damián focused his attention solely on Dellah now. His mind filtered out the image of the woman and replaced it with Mrs Hudson, his boss's wife. Attractive in a minimalist sort of way. Nothing out of the ordinary. Brown hair, a smattering of freckles across a flattened nose. Her lips were large though. He imagined kissing them, then blotted out the picture. Not the boss's wife.

"I'm a bit lost in all honesty, Damián. Can I help behind the desk today?" She felt herself shake momentarily, as though a wisp of air had passed over her.

He would have to move things. And remove things.

"Of course, Mrs Hudson, I'd be happy for the assistance."

Infamous

Trey opened the car door and stepped out. He had not meant to drive so fast. He would just get away with a warning this time, no harm done. After all, his mind was on other things. Apart from having to abandon the love of his life, Trey had just found out who his real mother was. This was something he had been working on finding out for several years. He had kept his findings quiet, even from Meghan, and that had been hard. Telling her could lead to disaster, and he needed to keep her at arm's length, for a while at least. The police officer seemed to size him up at first. Then he moved to flipping through a notebook.

"Have you been to this area before?" he asked Trey, who was shading his eyes from the blaring sun.

"Not before, no." Trey hesitated. "Did I do something wrong Officer?" he asked, trying to discern the outcome of the man's questioning.

"A little fast is all. There has been an incident near-by, we're monitoring the roads." The officer looked up from his notepad and eyed Trey. "You're very familiar sir, if you don't mind me saying."

"Not at all. You've probably seen me on TV. Is there anything I can do to help with the incident?" He sometimes used his fame to his advantage in situations like this.

"We have it under control, thanks all the same Mr Maguire. You keep up the day job, eh?" the officer said, smirking for the first time.

Trey smirked back and got back into his car. He started the engine and pulled away from the curb slowly, waving a spare hand at the officer. As his car drifted around the bend, he saw several Police cars dotted about the roadside. The Police were wandering the landscape, speaking into palm radios, and pointing down the embankment. Trey caught a glimpse of what seemed to be an abandoned BMW, its front bumper smashed and the driver side severely dented. He swerved to avoid another Police car coming in the opposite direction and looked to the road ahead. He felt relief to be finally on his way to finding out the truth about his past.

****

The car looked pretty messed up. Officer Logan had seen his fair share of accidents in his brief time on the Force but, without a doubt, this was the most stunning DOA he had ever laid eyes on. A passing motorcyclist had called it in and then sped off in the usual way they do around here. The less controversy they're involved with the better. Logan was the first to arrive and did all the usual checks, gloves on, tape up. Nothing suspicious in the first instance. It looked like she'd taken the turn too quickly and veered left to avoid something. That was his initial hypothesis. His boss was not so sure. Detective Viezmann had a sixth sense about these things. He had an inkling this was no accident.

So far, they had managed to keep the scene media-free, but they knew it wouldn't be long before the cameras rolled.

The woman had been identified by a card in her purse, 'Jinger Landley', and a few receipts from a hotel called The

Beverly. She had several pictures stuffed in there too and a cheque signed by a Mr Preston Hargreaves, also of The Beverly. Her phone was pretty smashed up, but the tech guys were working on finding her favourite numbers.

"Head there now Logan and just be aware," Viezmann breathed, "that hotel isn't for holidaymakers." He coughed painfully into his palm and wiped it on his jacket. Viezmann was not known for his sense of hygiene.

"What kind of hotel is it then, boss?" Logan asked, trying not to look too disgusted, but failing miserably.

"If you need somewhere to hide, and you're loaded," Viezmann shot Logan a glance, "The Beverly's where you go." He moved away from Logan and took in the devastation. The woman's body was being carefully removed and placed on a stretcher, ready to be taken for autopsy. Viezmann visibly shuddered.

"Always the pretty ones, eh boss?"

"Not always, Logan. Not always. Time to start finding out what really happened here." The Detective grumbled and walked silently to his car.

EPISODE TWO

The Sister

Jocelyn had spent her life trying to upstage her pretty and clever sister. And now she had finally pulled Jinger down from that high horse of hers. In order to get the man of your dreams, she realised, you must steal him from your twin sister.

Surely twins share the same dreams. Preston was incredibly attractive. She had always been drawn to outwardly attractive men and liked it especially if they were also inwardly attractive. Her needs had to be met. And when Jocelyn wanted someone, she got them, even if they had belonged to her sister. She had done it before, and she was sure she would do it again. Preston was just for now. Just until her sister moved on. Then she would too. It was a vicious circle, she knew that. But it was how she survived. Jinger was the eldest by five minutes. There had been complications with Jocelyn's birth and her time spent in intensive care as a new-born lasted until their first birthday, for which Jinger had a party. Their mother was quite willing to name favourites and saw her second born as exactly that, second. As much as she hated her mother and sister, Jocelyn couldn't help but love them also. She felt pain when her twin felt pain. Saw events through her sister's eyes, even if she was across the other side of the world. As siblings they had wanted for nothing, but Jocelyn felt she was owed everything. Right now, she could feel the agonising pain of loss, it was overwhelming and yet tinged with something else. It was as though Jinger had separated herself from her sister, their hearts were beating out of time. She looked at the clock on her mantelpiece. Four p.m. It was time to make the phone-call.

****

Preston Hargreaves looked solemnly at the door Jinger had walked out of. Five years they had been together. Five years of needing someone so badly every minute of every day. He had loved her from the moment their eyes met. A dinner party, something casual, a small group of people around a table. He remembered having a cigarette in his hand. Jinger stubbed out that habit. She was beautiful, intelligent, extraordinarily individual in her manners. And she smelt good too. He got up from the bed and walked to the bathroom, resting his hands on the sink. Her toothbrush lay by the tap. It was green, still wet. His eyes took on their own wetness and he couldn't shake off the substantial feeling of loneliness; it overwhelmed him, pressed down on his shoulders, made his body ache in bereavement. These feelings were very new to Preston. He was beginning to question himself and that was not something he had ever done. He caught his expression in the mirror. He looked drained; his skin was pale, languid. Lines decorated his forehead which seemed permanently furrowed. He tried a smile, but it seemed to pull at the dryness of his lips, its patheticness adding to the misery that consumed him. He missed her. And so did his smile. He regretted not saying so while he still had a chance. Any minute his phone would buzz. Play a tune she had chosen as his ringtone. Their song. But it wouldn't be her. He knew who it would be and yet, longed for the voice to say his name. Jocelyn. When he had first seen her, through the rear-view mirror of his car, he'd slammed down on his brakes. How could there be two such perfect women in this world? Jinge had mentioned her sister but not without a bad taste in her mouth. Preston had been fascinated, but Jinge had changed the subject quickly. Now he knew why.

He pulled away from his reflection, turned on the tap and splashed freezing water across his face. It revived him, enough to walk back to the bedroom and pick up his now ringing phone.

"Hello Preston. Is it safe to visit?"

****

The hotel lobby smelled strongly of lemons; the kind imported from the Amalfi coast. Sweet and refreshing. Warm and inviting. The Beverly's huge oak doors were wide open, allowing what was left of daylight to stream in and cascade off the gold parquet flooring. She moved slowly across it, her Jimmy Choos clacking loudly beneath a lime green maxi dress, toward the desk. The man behind it eyed her suspiciously at first then his expression turned to shock.

"I th...thought you said you would not be returning Ma'am?" he enquired, the colour draining from his face. The woman dipped her sunglasses, rested them on her nose and peered at him.

"Do I *know* you?" she replied.

"Er...you are here to see Mr Hargreaves I take it?" The man looked down at his screen, searching for an escape from her gaze.

"I am. Did he tell you? I'm Jocelyn." She extended her hand to him, but the man ignored it, obviously shaken.

"I'll head up then…" She turned on her heel and clacked all the way to the lift.

Damián lifted his gaze slightly. It was uncanny. This woman looked exactly like…but it was not her, that was for sure. He had made sure.

27

Jocelyn pressed the button for the lift and lifted her sunglasses off her nose. She smiled sweetly at the small, plump lady who joined in waiting for the lift. She was always ready with a smile and boy did she have a good smile. It was so much prettier than her sister's. Even their mother had commented on these differences in her children. The quick smile, the pale green eyes, the curly locks. The natural beauty. It took a lot to make Jinger smile; her eyes were brown and her hair, well, it was short and straight and boring in Jocelyn's mind. The lift pinged and the doors opened. The two women stepped inside, and Jocelyn smiled again.

"Which floor hon?" she asked, casually.

"Fourth thanks. I'm Candice, by the way. Nice to meet you."

"And you. I'm Jocelyn." She pressed the buttons for the fourth and fifth floors.

"You look so familiar, have you been in the hotel long?"

"I'm here to see a close friend. Perhaps you know him, Preston Hargreaves?"

"Oh, I think I do, yes. Here with his fiancée Jinny...or Jinger if I recall? Are you friends with her too?"

Jocelyn shifted uneasily.

"She's er...my er...sister."

She had not known they were engaged. The lift doors opened, and Candice smiled a goodbye. As they closed again, Jocelyn's heart began to race. The lift shot up and the doors flew open. She hesitated. She had never gone this far before. Before it had just been fun, taking them away from her oh so perfect sister. But now, she had broken up something real, something that had a future. She crossed herself and pressed the ground floor button. She pulled her phone out of her Prada bag and dialled a number. The phone rang once and then went straight through to voicemail.

"This is Jinger. I'm afraid I can't take your call at the minute. But please leave a message and I'll get back to you." The beep.

"Hey sis, I'm sorry. I didn't realise. You didn't tell me. He didn't tell me. I love you. I don't want this to damage things. Please ring me." She hung up the phone as the lobby reappeared. She stepped out and smiled sweetly at the concierge. He nodded as she left the hotel.

****

Preston eyed the door, his mobile phone clutched in one hand. He was not sure what to say to her or how to say it. How was it possible to love two women, especially sisters, especially twins? He walked to the window and pulled back the blind. The street outside the hotel was teeming with tourists, all heading towards the restaurant-end of town. He noticed that the sun was starting to set, its golden rays lapping the ocean waves. A figure was walking alone on the sands, her hair glistening in the half-light. He watched her as she stopped and turned to face the hotel. He caught something in her body language. She was smiling. His phone rang. The caller id was unfamiliar. He put it to his ear.

"Hello?"

"Mr Hargreaves?" The voice was male, unfeeling.

"Yes, how can I help?"

"I'm afraid I have some bad news."

****

The summer sunshine had gone, giving precedence to a cool breeze which lifted her skirts. The sand was soothing against the soles of her feet. She held a pair of Jimmy Choos in one hand. She looked over at The Beverly and saw lights dancing and heard music spilling out of the conservatory. She wondered if he was still there, sitting patiently in his room, waiting for her to knock on his door. He had not phoned her, not even left a message. Maybe he was not that bothered about her after all.

The Letter

Robyn held the envelope in her right hand. Her left was still shaking. It had arrived only moments ago, but her nerves were getting the better of her. It had been two long months since she had last spoken to her mother. Two months spent in the agony of the unknown. Her husband, Lonnie, was sitting staring at her across the room as though willing her to just open the damn thing. His patience was wearing thin. Robyn's brother, Preston, had not even replied to her phone message. She was beginning to doubt he even cared anymore; he always seemed so preoccupied with that Jinger woman. Robyn only put up with her because she was dating Preston, but he was stuck to this one like glue. Lonnie stood up and walked to her, kneeling at her feet and pressing his hand into hers.

"Don't open it," he muttered unconvincingly.

"Don't contradict yourself Lon. Only yesterday you were asking when this would arrive and now, you're not bothered?"

"Of course, I'm bothered. I'd love to know what's in there. But it's your letter. You must make the decision." His eyes were tired. They had spent most of the night arguing. It was becoming a regular participant in their marriage.

"I want you to be there for me if I do. I need you so much Lonnie." Robyn squeezed his hand and he brought hers up to his lips, kissing it lightly and then letting it go. This type of affection had been absent for so long; he wasn't sure how to bring it back.

"Whatever it says, we deal with it together. I promise." he said, standing and walking back to his chair. Lonnie had found the past months unbearable. He had done everything for his wife; his shoulder was heavy with her tears. He sat again and forced himself to smile. Robyn took hold of the envelope in both hands and looked intently at the handwriting. It was her mother's. No-one knew it was here, that she had it. She turned it over and began to slowly tear it open. Time had taken a deep breath. Everything around Robyn faded as her eyes focussed on the one thing her mother had left. Being careful not to damage the contents, her fingers suddenly faltered. Her heart began to thump heavily in her chest, each beat getting louder in her ears as she finally eased the contents from the envelope. She let it fall to her feet as she opened the sheet, glancing at the words over and over so as not to miss one. She looked up at Lonnie whose smile had all but disappeared and in its place a sense of relief had settled over him. A weight had been lifted.

"It reads as I thought it would. It's finished Lonnie. My mother's secret is out."

Memories

She had decided to write everything down. Right from the beginning. When they met, it was as though lightning had hit them both simultaneously. He was standing across a crowded room. That old cliché, love at first sight. She hadn't believed it until then. She stared at the photograph in front of her. Their first holiday together. They had gone to Malaga, on the coast of Spain. He had wanted to see the ancient sights, remnants of a forgotten time; she had wanted to sunbathe. How pathetic that sounded now. How much she wished she could jump into that picture and feel close to him again. He loved history so much. He loved finding out new things, discovering architecture and burial sites. His major was archaeology and he'd spent so much time at ruins and digs. Her pencil nib snapped. She threw it across the room and sobbed. Her body ached all over. Trey had gone. She wanted to rip the photograph, tear up the memories and throw them away. Meghan pulled a blanket around her shoulders and sat shivering on the oak panelled floor of *her* house. She had to call it that now because he had gone. 'Her house,' it sounded so final. She looked at the words she had written through bitter tears.

****

Trey had wanted to call her since he arrived. His first instinct was to grab his mobile and press one on the speed dial, just to tell her he'd arrived safely. But he hadn't even told her where he'd gone. He threw his phone onto the motel bed and knelt to unpack his satchel. The papers lay strewn across the floor. He had looked over them countless times, recounting his memories, as far back as he could go, trying to pinpoint the exact moment it happened. He zipped up the satchel and threw himself on the bed to stare at the ceiling. He was sick of looking at words. He wanted to see pictures, photographs, something more aesthetically pleasing. He dug his hand into his jean pocket and pulled out a crumpled piece of paper. He unfolded it, working out the creases, until he could see her face clearly in front of him. It had been their first holiday together. He had been selfish. He wanted to see history and she wanted to relax. They were both laughing, looking at each other. He remembered holding the camera in front of them and saying 'say cheese' loudly. Meghan had started giggling and it just set him off. It was a perfect moment. Recorded just for times like this. It was starting to get dark outside. He could do no more until the morning. For now, he needed to rest. He pulled the duvet around his body and fell into a deep and mournful sleep.

The Saviour

Candice liked staying at the hotel. This was her seventh visit in four years. The anonymity it gave her was so refreshing after a fractious period in her life. To maintain this quietude, Candice had placed a hold on her room. The Beverly allowed its guests to use the same suite every time they visited, for an exorbitant fee of course. Having a balcony that overlooked the ocean, a separate bedroom and living area both with cinema screens, as well as a modern kitchen and grandiose bathroom, complete with jacuzzi, was all she needed.

She planned to have an eighth stay just before Christmas. Her first husband had booked this exact hotel for their one-year anniversary, and she had continued the tradition. Her second husband had hated coming here initially, but he was starting to allow himself to get some enjoyment out of it. After all, the bar stayed open late, and she was paying for it. She kicked her shoes off and walked casually across the Umbrian grey sandstone floor of their apartment suite towards the balcony. The triple-glazed partition doors were already ajar to allow the cool air to drift inside. She breathed it in and leaned against the balustrade, her back to the ocean view. A half-empty glass of vino in hand, Candice felt her body relax. She could not imagine being happier than this.

Carlos nursed his pint of very strong ale and eyed up a female customer. She smiled at him sardonically and moved to sit with a very stern looking male. He nodded to the young bartender for a fresh one and threw the rest down his throat. Carlos had been used to rejection from an incredibly early age. His own parents had abandoned him; his only option was to live with an aging aunt who plied him with biscuits and cups of tea. No wonder he turned to alcohol. But then he met Candice. She had been married before but so much had gone wrong that really, they ended up saving each other. They were very much a separate couple, preferring time on their own rather than together. But when they were together, chemistry kicked in. It was more passion than he had ever known, and he loved her so much more for it. Over the years, Carlos had kicked various drug habits and come out the other end a better man for it. If it weren't for Candice, he knew he'd be right back at the beginning. She gave him a reason to stay clean. He sipped at the freshly poured pint and decided it was time to retire for the night. He pictured her now, curled up on the balcony, a book in one hand, a glass of wine in the other, the night air lifting strands of her auburn hair. He loved watching her when she didn't know he was there. He stood and swayed slightly; his head alive with the alcohol. He would watch her tonight, just for a little while. Carlos headed towards the door that led back into the hotel reception.

****

Damián looked at the clock on his computer screen. Quarter past midnight. His shift had finished over an hour ago, but Meghan still hadn't turned up. He began to shuffle uneasily in his chair. He needed to leave. He watched the gentleman head, unsteadily, towards the lift. He'd always found it fascinating that there was only one lift in this hotel. All the other hotels he'd worked in had at least half a dozen; people constantly going back and forth, up, and down in cycles. It did, however, make it easier for him to keep track of who came and went in The Beverly. He'd been instructed to keep watch. And now Mr Chambers was making his way back to his wife. He needed to move quickly. Then, footsteps. He looked up into the tired eyes of his new boss.

"Damián? Get yourself away, son. I'll keep an eye until Meghan gets here. Traffic apparently."

"Are you sure sir?" Damián tried to hide his agitation.

"Off you go. Take an hour off your shift tomorrow too." He ushered Damián out of his seat and plonked himself down, heavily, on the chair. Damián smiled quickly and gathered his belongings.

"Thank you, sir. See you tomorrow."

He rushed out of the hotel doors to the side car park. He got silently into his car, his hands holding the wheel. He had to do something. He certainly could not let this one go.

Damián had always done as he was told, and why should now be an exception? He gently opened his car door and closed it with a sigh. The night was still young...

EPISODE THREE

Unhappy Families

Lonnie watched his wife from the window. She had decided to visit her brother, a bloke Lonnie could not respect. They had had their fair share of arguments and even a physical fight, which Lonnie remembered winning. He still felt the ache in his knuckles and his head thumped with the memory of Preston's left foot. Robyn had not forgiven either of them. And he was not sure he could forgive her. He was her husband. They were supposed to be a team, to support each other yet, she still stuck by her idiot brother. Preston did not deserve to know about the letter. He would want it all for himself, all the praise for finding the truth and then he would tell his current partner.

She was gorgeous. Lonnie had noticed. He could not help but. He loved his wife, but it was fine to look, right? He smiled at the thought of Jinger and then caught sight of Robyn pulling out of the long drive. The car was spattered with mud. He should have cleaned it, but surely Robyn had not noticed. Her mind was certainly focused elsewhere. The car disappeared, and he turned from the window, heading to his study. He knew what he would be faced with. A room filled solely with disappointment. Lonnie had tried to keep afloat but now he was drowning, breathing in water. He had not meant for things to get this far. He pushed hard on the door, and it swung open, the handle smacking into an already bruised wall. How many times had he been here? He told Robyn the first time and she had helped him out, God love her. Then the second and the third. After that he had told her he was through. No more gambling, no more debts. And at the time, he held onto that. Then an offer he just could not refuse landed on his desktop. His heart skipped several beats before he had clicked and responded. Now it was too late to ask for help. He would have to start to clean up his own mess.

****

Robyn scanned the road ahead. It was always a quiet neighbourhood. This was one of the reasons they chose to move here. Nothing much seemed to happen. She liked it that way. Except now. Her brother needed to know what the letter said. His name was all over it. She knew her mother and knew how much she loved Preston. It had all been a game to her from the start, a game without instructions, a game where the rules did not apply. She caught a glimpse of her face in the rear-view mirror. Her eyes were shaded and slightly creased at the edges. No hint of the joy that used to sit there. There were new lines etched on her forehead; born from the difficulties she had faced these past months. Her hair had never looked worse. Greys overtaking the once lush blonde. She focused back on the road but noticed a car creeping steadily up behind her. She always kept to speed limits but suddenly felt inclined to press down harder on the accelerator. Probably completely innocent, she thought and followed the signs for The Beverly.

Truths and Lies

Preston gripped the phone. He was unable to process the conversation he had just had. Not only had he just said goodbye to the love of his life, but she had gone, for good. The police officer said it was instant. She would not have felt any pain. But he did. A deep gnawing, biting feeling inside his chest. His stomach swirling, a knife-slice through his heart. Jinge was gone. Jinge was dead. Her smell still lingered in the room, so how could she be? He dropped the phone at his feet and stared at the now blank screen. "What am I supposed to do without you?" he murmured, "God-damn you!"

A tap, tap on the door seemed to bring him back from the edge of the cliff he stood on.

"Preston, it's me, Robyn." His sister's voice, comforting, calming, close.

"It's open," he returned, not moving from the edge of the bed. The door clicked and opened slowly. Robyn always took her time; she never rushed anything. Preston was the complete opposite. He could not hang around and wait. He stood, regaining his self-awareness. He was a doer, not a thinker. Action. Got to get on, move on.

She stood in the doorway, staring at her little brother. She knew instantly that something had happened. Something bad.

"Where's Jinger?" she asked, taking a few steps towards him. He had stood up, just as she walked in, but she knew from his body language that it was not good news.

"On the way to the Morgue, I guess."

Robyn pulled back and began to shake.

"What? I mean...how?" She could not find the right words to fit the situation. A situation she had not predicted. Her thoughts driving to The Beverly had not included this.

"She's dead, Bobby. I just...I just ended it, she left and now...she's dead." Preston's face started to crumple, his eyes filling like huge rock pools; Jinger's face swimming in them, clouding them; she was all encompassing, all he wanted and all he'd lost. He started breathing rapidly, sat down on the bed, and then stood up.

Robyn wanted to move to his side, but her body would not go. She hated this sort of thing. She was no good at comfort. Hugs were not her forte.

"I don't know how I…can I do anything Pres?" His lips were quivering, he looked like a toddler after a tantrum, all red eyed and pouting.

"She's dead, Bobby. There's nothing anyone can do." He sniffed back his tears and sucked in a breath. "What are you doing here anyway? It's been a while, sis."

It had been two years. Two years since the bust up between him and Lonnie. Two years of hearing how messed up Preston was, how she should be supporting her husband not her stupid child of a brother. The argument had been nothing to begin with; just Lonnie being on edge about work and taking it out on Preston. In all honesty, Robyn knew he was jealous of him. Preston had everything Lonnie didn't - good looks, youth, beautiful girls on his arm, charm, and intelligence. He also had money. A lot of money. Robyn and Preston had different fathers, but their bond was still strong because of their mother. Preston's father had been wealthy, and this was one of the reasons why their mother had been so drawn to him. He had owned the hotel they now stood in and, before he passed away, he wrote a new will leaving everything to Preston. However, he did not want the hotel; he did not want to be tied down to something, so, he sold it. And made a fortune doing so. Preston was savvy and Lonnie really wasn't. Robyn sometimes forgot why she married him. There must have been something that drew her to this lost soul, something real that made her love him for so long. Love was still there but in a unique way. A way that meant they lived as one but separately. They smiled as they passed each other now. They used to kiss. They shook hands when a decision was made. They used to make love.

Robyn looked across at her now desolate brother.

"It's mum," she said, "I got the letter."

Fake News

When Dellah Ramsey became a journalist, she had found her true calling in life. From a small-town rag to a big town publication, she pushed her way through the ranks until her name hit the big time. She loved being recognised in the streets for her diverse and witty opinions and dialogue. People wanted to be interviewed by her. They knew her style and liked it. To be in one of Dellah Ramsey's write-ups was to make it in this world.

She smirked at the headline on the local tell-all and placed it back on her husband's desk. She could never write for a magazine which exploited people and besmirched reputations for entertainment. It was unethical. The photograph of the three Hudsons, framed in what she would call cheap tat, stared back at her from the wall above Mitchell's file cabinet. Randy was a strong and determined five-year-old now, not the sweet and jam-covered baby he once was. She always thought Mitchell looked unhappy in that photo. His face was drawn in a very straight line. No smiles. He said it had been a long day, he had not wanted to stand around having photos taken but Dellah had insisted. She wanted to show the world her perfect family.

****

Mitchell had been in meetings all morning. His head was stinging with the politics of it all. Running a hotel was harder than he could ever have imagined, especially The Beverly. Everything had to be run past 'The Board,' something his predecessor set up when he thought his son was taking the reins. Unfortunately for Mitchell, there was no getting rid of them any time soon. He rubbed roughly at his temples as he walked from the conference room, a space bigger than any meeting room he had ever known before. Its ceilings hung with chandeliers; cloisters of architraves decorating the high windows which framed some of the most impressive views of the bay beyond. Mitchell liked the way the room fell away from you as you walked in, making your presence paramount. Of course, his clients had no interest in the behind-the-scenes goings on, as long as their rooms were licked clean and gourmet food was on tap, they were placated. He was always amazed at how incredibly wealthy they all were. Some seemed to have an endless supply of money. He guessed that his nose should stay firmly out of their business as long as they kept paying his never-ending bills. He headed towards his office where he knew Dellah would be waiting, twiddling her thumbs to keep from staying still. She needed to get back to work but he worried for her. Her last story had devastating consequences and without this move, who knew where she would be now? He reached his office door and took some deep breaths before walking in, pasting a superlative smile on his not so content face.

"Dellah, darling. Shall we get dinner?"

The Eye of the Storm

The wine bottle was empty. The glass next to it was full. A lipstick stain, iridescent pink, kissed the rim. She had fixed her eyes on the distant shore. She was waiting for the sun to rise. The beach below the balcony stretched out towards an ocean which seemed at rest. Yet, her heart still drummed in her ears. Carlos had done it again. She knew she needed to forgive him and help him. All she ever did was forgive but she could never forget. Her hand caressed the silver pendant at her throat. The cold metal sent a shiver through her fingers. Some feeling at least from the one thing he had bought for her. Candice was no fool. She knew who he was when she met him. She knew his past and she wanted so badly to be a part of his future. The present was the issue; the only thing that made her heart race and her mind whirl. There was a storm coming and not just the one hanging over her relationship. The wind whipped up and stung her cheeks. She wanted to wait it out, but the air became too harsh, too penetrative. She stood and backed into the comfort of their room. The room she shared with Carlos. Carlos who had not yet returned. Carlos who was drinking again. Carlos who needed her more than she needed him.

****

As Carlos stumbled from the lift, he collided with a water fountain and felt his head spin.

"Are you well, Sir?" asked a familiar voice.

He tried to focus but his eyes filled with water, so he rubbed them impulsively.

"Been better," he joked, trying to work out the owner of the voice.

A figure moved towards him; its face a group of lines and shadows, two piercing specks where eyes should have been.

"Can I help you to your room?" it asked gently, reaching out what he assumed was a hand.

Suddenly something gripped him, something strong, stronger than he had ever felt. He couldn't fight it. Lights filled his eyes and a smell filtered rapidly up his nostrils to fill his head with darkness.

****

The figure smirked and dragged the body to a small linen cupboard at the end of the corridor. Proud to be so strong. Proud to remove things that were useless. Because what a waste to the world they were.

EPISODE FOUR

Lost

Trey's journey had been a long one. He knew where he needed to be, but getting there was tough. Not only was Meghan playing games with his mind, but his mother's wishes were tugging at his heart. He had always, always, wanted to meet the woman. He had heard stories, of course. His adoptive parents were never silent about his origins. But he felt that they held the most important thing back. Why did she leave him?

He gazed at the road in front and turned the stereo up to drown out his thoughts. Her letter said she would be waiting for him, in the lake house. A house he had been to before, with his parents. How did she know about the lake house? The road veered right and there was the sign he'd been waiting for. He flicked his indicator and steered towards it, gently pressing the break.

This road started to become so familiar to him that he smiled at the memory of it. It took him down through a great expanse of trees, their leaves shading him from the blinding sun. Then suddenly fields spread out before him, dense and thick, as warming to him as the summer of his childhood. He breathed them in and waited for the view he knew from his dreams.

The Lake. It stretched out further than his imagination would ever take him. A deep, blue, iridescent water. Home.

He started to slow his car; he could see the house, its thick wooden walls washed clean by the purity of the air. They shone in the sunlight which bounced effortlessly off the lake, right into his eyes.

****

Meghan Brock was right where she needed to be, behind the desk inputting the details of The Beverly's newest resident. She enjoyed chatting to her clients and they obviously enjoyed talking to her too. She had a way with people. She wasn't naive; she knew that the hotel residents weren't flawless. But this was her job, and she was damn good at it.

"Er, excuse me please!" a voice said urgently, forcing its way to the front of the queue.

Meghan looked up into a pair of worried eyes.

"My husband didn't come back last night; please tell me you've seen him?!"

"Mrs Chambers, is it?"

"Candice is fine. Have you seen him? I've been phoning him since sunrise. And with the storm last night...I just...I hope he wasn't..."

"I've not long been here Mrs Chambers, but I can easily find out if anyone has seen him. Please, give me a moment and take a seat in the lobby."

Candice was visibly shaking, her hands caught up in front of her. She had not changed out of her smart clothes and her hair had begun to loosen itself from a once-tight ponytail. She turned from the desk and felt herself float to the lobby, throwing herself down on the plush gold chaise long and praying for news. The news could be good or bad, as long as it was news.

Meghan turned her attention to the next client, hastily typing an email to Damián whilst also confirming their booking. She hoped he had seen Mr Chambers; a scandal at The Beverly was not something she wanted to be involved with. Guests did not just go missing. Her phone buzzed and she glanced at the screen. Trey.

Home is where the Hate Is

Lonnie wasn't in the mood for seeing him. When he first saw the car pull into their drive, he felt relief that she was home, but she was not alone. The passenger door opened and bang, there he was. Preston. What the hell was he doing here?!

They stared at each other across the living room, hating the sight, longing to take the first punch. Robyn stood between the two men in her life and knew she could never choose, not when the chips were down, not even if her life depended on it. She sucked in a breath and then began.

"Our mother wants us to find him. It's important to her."

Preston took his focus from Lonnie and moved his gaze to his big sister.

"Where is she, Bobby? Where did she go?" His nickname for Robyn had always riled Lonnie, but he kept his cool this time. He knew Preston's game and he wasn't about to let him win.

"Mum had to take some time away from this. She couldn't face things."

"She always was weak," spat Preston "But where exactly did she take off to? Some island somewhere? A place for quitters?" He was getting angrier now and only Robyn knew how to cool him off.

"Mum didn't tell me where, Pres, but she needed you to know she loves you and the money you gave her is still safe. She hasn't touched a dime."

He needed to believe her. The money was what kept him sane. He could not survive without it to cushion his fall.

Lonnie stood now and moved to place an arm around his wife's shoulders. He felt her flinch at the touch. She looked up at him and then back to her brother.

"How's that girlfriend of yours, Preston?" Lonnie broached the elephant; he had already seen the news.

Silence fell on the room. A painful silence. It seeped into the walls and crept up their skin. Each shivered involuntarily.

"*Jocelyn* is well, thanks Lonnie." The first words Preston had directed at his brother-in-law were full to the brim of spite. His voice was thick with it.

"I think it's time to find him. He needs to know. We need to know if what mum said is real." Robyn shook off her husband's arm and knelt in front of Preston, placing her hands on his knees.

"Let's do this together, just us. I have his number." The siblings caught each other's eyes and could see their reflections; their mother's features echoed in their own.

Preston took his sister's hands and nodded.

"Just us," he said.

A Point of No Return

Jocelyn had made up her mind. And there was no going back. She still felt she could not be with Preston, not when her sister had gone that extra step and was wearing his ring. She wondered how he had proposed. Some grand gesture, down on one knee with the sun setting behind them and champagne spilling from their flutes. She thought about when he had proposed. Had he come to see Jocelyn afterwards, or just before? Had he told her he loved her before he proposed to her sister? The questions swam incessantly in her head. No matter how many times she tried to focus on something else, there they were. Preston and Jinger. Hand in hand. A diamond glittering on her finger.

She stared at herself in the long mirror, admiring the waves in her hair, how taught and smooth her skin was, how graceful her body seemed. She had chosen green again, a playsuit to show off her legs, dappled with blossoms and interweaving vines; she really suited green. It was a match made in heaven, if there really was such a thing. She loved looking at her own reflection. It made her feel powerful, strong. Yet ever since she had left The Beverly, something had seemed off to her. Something was missing. She just could not work out what. She slumped down on her hard, motel bed and grabbed the controller. Her fingers caressed the buttons, flicking through the channels without really noticing the TV screen. Then, she dropped it. Her sister's face was staring back at her. A headline moved steadily underneath. 'No Witnesses,' 'Suspicious circumstances,' '...tampered with.'

Her mind began to race, images of her sister smiling, laughing turned quickly to her body, cold, unmoving, lifeless. Jocelyn screamed.

Hearts and Minds

The house was empty. No furniture, fixtures, or fittings. Absolutely no sign that anyone had stayed there or had even visited recently. He slumped down on the wooden floor and put his head in his hands. It was time to give up. His road had come to a dead end. Trey felt so far from the truth now, if there even was any truth. The letter he received said she would be here waiting for him. His mother. The one who had given him life. Well now she had taken it away. He had lost Meghan and, he realised, she was the only truth he needed.

He had expected something from his mother. Some inkling that she had been here. Even the smell of what he imagined her perfume to be like. He looked to the window he had stood at as a child, eagerly awaiting his father's return from the Lake. His father had been gone for five years, a pain that stayed with him, especially now.

He stood and dusted himself down, pulling his mobile out of his trouser pocket. He swiped the screen and was faced with Meghan, beaming back at him. He dialled her number, fingers trembling. Trey prayed she would answer this time. Her voice would bring him back to his senses. It rang. Twice.

Silence.

The Bond that Binds Us

The hotel had never seen so many people through its doors. People falling over each other just to ask questions. Cameras clicking, snapping everywhere. Shouts echoing around its thick marble walls. Everyone wanted to see Preston Hargreaves. Most of the guests had checked out, preferring to hide from The Beverly rather than in it.

Officer Logan strolled casually through the masses and headed for the reception. He leant gingerly on the counter and waited until the woman caught his eye. She had a telephone to her ear and was nodding, rapidly. She placed her hand on the receiver.

"We're a little understaffed today, Officer. If you wouldn't mind waiting?"

She continued the nodding conversation she was having but Logan didn't move. He found the whole thing fascinating. Of course, he had heard of The Beverly, but to be standing inside it, well that was a real reality check.

There were hardly any pictures on the walls, he noticed. He guessed not many guests spent time in the lobby, it would just be a sort of in-between place for them; certainly, nowhere to hide in here. He spotted the woman's name badge. Meghan.

"I need to speak with the manager. Immediately." he said, not really caring that he was interrupting her.

She nodded and pointed towards a door in the far corner of the lobby. It was huge, bordered by thick panels painted with gold leaf. The sign which was attached read *General Manager* and was written in an imposing script. Someone was trying too hard, thought Logan. He shrugged and wandered over, his shoes squeaking on the tiled floor. He was sure it wasn't usually this dirty. He knocked hard and waited for a response.

****

Mitchell had switched off his phone. He could not deal with any more of the absurdity aimed at his hotel. A car crash, that is what had led to all this. What did it have to do with

The Beverly anyway? He knew who Jinger Landley was, she was Preston's fiancée. He knew because Preston had told him he was going to propose and needed to make everything perfect. Mitchell had gone all out for the old boss's son. Candles, champagne, an oversized tee pee on the beach, violinists, you name it Mitchell had sourced it. He felt a twinge of sadness for Preston's loss, but the anger was spilling over about the effect on his hotel.

The knock on his door made him jump. He had sent Dellah to the hotel Spa, and insisted that he not be disturbed.

"Yes? Who is it?"

"Officer Logan, from downtown. I need a word, Mr Hudson."

Mitchell smoothed down his hair and adjusted his tie.

"Please, come in, Officer," he said, and the door swung open.

****

Damián had slipped into reception unnoticed by his colleagues. Meghan had gone over to the far foyer, her arms wrapped around a young woman in obvious distress. He had begun to sweat. There were too many journalists here. This was not how it was supposed to be. The phone was ringing incessantly behind the counter. He sat down behind the desk and pasted on his smile.

"Good afternoon. You're through to The Beverly. Damián speaking, how can I be of assistance?"

****

Dellah watched from a doorway as Damián appeared through the crowds and sat down at reception. She watched as he began to smile at no-one. She had just had some quiet time in the Spa, time to think things through while a masseuse eased her physical and emotional aches. Her forefinger scratched at her thumb, and she made her way towards her husband's office. The door was ajar, and she heard voices coming from inside. One, Mitchell's, gruff and defensive; the other she did not recognise, condescending, wilful. She knocked gently and smiled as the two men faced her.

"Dellah, my love, please come on in." Mitchell ushered her towards a chair. "This is my wife. Dellah, this is Officer Logan. I'd like her to sit in on this if you don't mind."

"Of course, we're only having a friendly chat, aren't we?" Logan looked Dellah up and down, appraisingly.

"So, Mr Hargreaves is in residence, then?" Logan continued.

"As I said, Preston comes and goes. I don't know if he's here or not." Mitchell was holding on tightly to his patience.

"You do have logbooks, cameras? We could have a look now?" Logan was pushing.

"You'd need an extraordinarily strong warrant for that, Officer. The Beverly is a safe haven, not everybody wants to be seen." Mitchell sat in his chair and placed his hands on the desk in front of him.

"I am but a vessel, Officer. The guests here come and go as they please. Now, if there isn't anything else…"

Dellah stirred slightly in her chair. Logan did not speak. Just smiled. A sardonic smile. He would be back. They both knew it.

Mitchell waited. He was good at that. The Officer nodded then turned to leave.

"Oh, one more thing, Mr Hudson…if you don't mind," Logan turned back. "You'll need to stop anyone else entering the building from now on."

Mitchell cursed as he left.

****

Carlos coughed. A deep, rasping cough. He needed air. The fresh kind. He was in a dark place. It was hot. Stuffy. He felt around for a lifeline. His head buzzing, ears singing. His foot was stuck under something heavy, so he tried to lift it. He was sure he was lifting material. He leant forward to smell it and knew exactly where he was. Now to find the door.

EPISODE FIVE

The Rough with the Smooth

Meghan held Candice as her mother once held her. Close. She needed reassurance after the tragedy of the day. Just because one person had died did not mean her husband had too. He was an alcoholic, she said. He could have wandered off, Meghan insisted. Best to wait it out. She touched her face and smiled gently.

"Let's get you to your room. Run a bath and I'll send up some room service. Complimentary of course."

Candice looked at her comforter through hooded eyes.

"You're right. I'm probably just being over-cautious. Thank you, Meghan. Thank you for just…for being here."

Meghan took her hands and helped her up, guiding her over to the lift and walking her into it.

"I'll be fine now, honestly," Candice sniffed, "but don't forget that room service…" she mumbled as the lift doors closed.

Meghan laughed inwardly. It was the first time in days she had laughed. She took her mobile out of her pocket and looked again at the screen. One missed call. Trey. Better late than never, she thought, and returned the call. It rang once before it was answered. His voice was music.

"Meghan. I love you, please forgive me."

She was not sure if she could. She looked back towards the lift, remembering Candice. How easily she came around. Meghan knew it was going to be ok.

"Come home," she said and hung up the phone.

****

For so long The Beverly had been a retreat for those needing an escape from life, the universe and everything in between. It was a haven for tax fraudsters. It was a warm place at the end of a messy and costly divorce. But also, its exclusivity meant you were safe from the media spotlight, safe from the world outside its privileged walls.

But now, the once flawless hotel car park was littered with sandwich boxes, crisp packets, and chocolate wrappers. Plastic bottles rattled across the pristine concrete. The media were here. Cameras lifted from boots, clicked, and checked. Notebooks flicked through. Dictaphones pressed against eager ears, 'Did I get anything there?' murmured one voice, 'I'm sure he said...' grumbled another. The Beverly was no longer what it had been. And Mitchell Hudson was treading water.

A Present from the Past

Dellah scrolled through the emails on her phone. Randy had made a nuisance of himself again at school and she had had enough of dealing with it. She hit *forward-to* and typed Mitchell's personal email in. Let him sort this one out. She was expecting something from an old colleague of hers from her halcyon days; Emilia Gonzalez still had connections within the haze of the media industry and must know something beyond what had been reported. So much had come out about Preston Hargreaves' littered past, his family, father, and his womanising, but nothing about the one undoubtedly missing piece in this complex jigsaw.

Years and years had passed since she had interviewed Damián. Ten, perhaps, although so much had happened in between, it could have been more. She was so much younger then, full of the joie de vivre of youth, the effervescence of innocence. Her first job had been taking messages for the editor of the tabloid she would eventually call home. When the time came to write her first article, Meghan had been blown away by how incredible it felt to see her name in print. She had gone by a different name then, her hair was streaked blonde, and she wore coloured contacts. She had wanted a new persona, to hide away from the name that had given her so much grief as a child. So, there was no way he knew who she was now. She had had to hide her identity plenty of times. But the final time was the last straw for her publication. Delilah had found out too much and it hurt people, people who had a standing, people whose money held sway in the highest places. It had been time to step down and move away. That is when she had become complacent and when the other troubles began. Her hand hovered over the keyboard. There was one other person she could ask. It was a risk. She scratched her forefinger with her thumb nail and nibbled at her bottom lip. High risk or not, she had no options left.

****

Trey cruised towards The Beverly. His heart felt light again. The way it used to feel when Meghan first came into his life. He started to slow when he noticed the cameras. All eyes turned to him, and bright lights flashed through his windscreen. He brought the car to a stop. At the touch of a button his window slid down and he stuck his head into the limelight.

"I'm just visiting my girlfriend at work, guys. No need for all the hysteria!" Trey liked to charm the paparazzi; he was well known for it.

"Hey Mr Maguire! Trey, isn't it? Have you not heard?" one reporter goaded, stepping towards his car door, surreptitiously.

Trey had been so long in the darkness that the world around him had not existed. Even the spotlight he had relied on for so long, had faded into the background of his need to find the truth.

"I'm behind on the news I'm afraid but I'm sure Meghan will catch me up!" He pulled up the window then slipped his car past the buzz in the car park. He found a spot around the corner, a place he liked to park when he was dropping Meghan at work. It was secluded. He smiled at the memories that came flooding back. Every thought he had of her made his chest swell with longing. He gripped the steering wheel and squeezed it in his palms. She was waiting for him, and he needed her so badly.

Family Ties

Robyn was sitting in reception. She had crossed and uncrossed her legs several times before deciding to stand and walk around instead. Her brother said he would meet her down here, but she had been waiting for longer than ten minutes. The manager appeared to have brought in more security, so the media had begun to dissipate leaving only their messy footprints behind. Several of the hotel's cleaners were hard at work, mops and buckets sloshing soapy water over the tiles. Robyn steered clear and checked her watch. As she began to pace, a young gentleman walked through the doors and headed straight for the young receptionist. They embraced passionately then coyly retreated into an alcove, away from prying eyes. Robyn could not help but stare. There was something urgently familiar about the man. Tall, black haired, stubbled cheeks and a strongly rounded chin. His eyes were locked into the receptionist's. Eyes so like Robyn's. Their passion was palpable. Robyn knew him. She had always known him. It hit her like a bullet from a gun. Winded her. Instinct kicked in and she headed their way. The lift doors opened and out stepped Preston looking a little worse for wear. He intercepted her before she reached the alcove and wrapped his arms around her.

"Thank God you're here Bobby! It's all such a mess! They think I did something to Jinge! Me? I loved her Bobby; I bloody loved her!" he sobbed into her collar, and she writhed under him, eventually releasing herself. Robyn did not do hugs.

"I know. The police will work out the truth. Everything will be back to normal in no time at all."

She moved back from him, attempting to keep her distance but he tried to fall on her again, needing his sister's comfort. Robyn reluctantly dropped her hands onto his shoulders but turned her attention back to the young man. The couple had vanished.

EPISODE SIX

The Phone-call

Lonnie's hands were itchy. He could not sit still. He had been up and down like a kid's bouncy ball all afternoon. An empty whiskey bottle eyed him from across the room. The glass was still full, however, and he picked it up and threw the hot liquid down his throat. He winced then shuddered. Enough for today. It had initially been for courage, the courage to tell his wife how much difficulty they were in. But she had not come home yet. He had no idea where she was. The car keys hung temptingly on the peg by the front door. He shook his head, not just to dissuade the dizziness and nausea that was beginning to creep in but to stop himself from making yet another big mistake. Instead, he picked up his mobile and swiped it into life. He pressed one and speed-dialled Robyn. No time like the present.

"Lonnie, I'm in the middle of something." Robyn's rapid response had startled him.

"Sorry, hun. I just...I really need to talk to you." He was slurring, he knew.

"Lonnie, you're drunk again. Phone me when you're sober."

She hung up. He collapsed to the floor and wept like a baby.

****

Robyn had sent Preston back to his apartment and was waiting it out in the lobby. Things had quietened down now; bulky security guards stood like centurions at the front entrance. She had not seen the like before.

Damián had been eyeing her from the front desk, fascinated by this woman who would not leave. Robyn had noticed him too and they fixed gazes.

"Will the young, female receptionist be coming back?" she inquired across the expanse of the foyer.

Damián stood and motioned to her. She approached him and slipped behind the desk. He pointed at his screen, in particular a couple shrouded in darkness.

"Ah, I'd rather not look, if you don't mind." she said and moved away. She noticed he was smirking, rather unpleasantly, and felt extremely uncomfortable being next to him.

"You're more than welcome to continue to wait." he sneered, obviously enjoying her discomfort.

"I'll head home and come back later, but thanks anyway." Robyn turned quickly from him and squeezed her way through Security and towards a huge sense of freedom. She noted his name in her memory, *Damián*.

After the conversation with Lonnie, she had put her phone in her bag, removing it from her sight, something she wanted to do with her husband. She knew he had been up to his old tricks again, but her mind had been too focussed on finding her long-lost brother to deal with his idiocy. Yes, now she knew who he was. The gentleman who walked into The Beverly; the boy her mother gave away.

The Mother

She had watched as his car pulled away. She had watched as it sped down the lane, away from her again.

Her emotions were a rollercoaster, making her queasy. The letters had arrived, then. They had been read and digested. The first steps had been taken and now the ride was about to start.

She looked out over the lake and breathed in the cool summer air. He had been happy here and that made her happy. Some feeling seemed to tug at her heart. She forced it down and decided to use her head instead.

Melissa had so many secrets and she just could not hold onto them all anymore. Her spinning plates were beginning to wobble and, if she did not move quickly, they would start to fall and smash to smithereens.

Her daughter would already be on the scent. She knew Robyn so well; so, like her father, never one to hold back. When she wanted something, she would work damn hard to get it. And it did not matter how long it took. Preston was more like his mother, erratic, unstable. Melissa saw only her bad traits in her eldest son. Already, he was under investigation for his fiancée's murder. Oh yes, she had read the news. When she saw his name, her heart skipped a few beats. She certainly would not put it past him. The apple had not fallen far. He had always been an over-emotional wreck.

After a few more breaths of the soothing air, Melissa stooped down into her Merc and rested some dark glasses on her nose. It was about time to show face.

The Reunion

Someone was banging urgently on her apartment door. She sat up in the bath and waited. The banging continued.

"Yes? Is it room service?" she inquired a little briskly, drawing the bubbles over her naked self.

"Candice? Are you in there?"

Carlos's voice boomed through the room. She pushed herself up quickly, clambering from the slickness of the bath and grabbing a towel.

"I'm coming darl, I'm coming!" She ran to the door and slid the bolt. Just as she grabbed the handle, the door flew open, and he caught her up in his embrace. Their mouths hungry for each other.

"You smell of laundry detergent," she giggled.

"I'll explain later." he moaned, throwing her onto their bed.

****

Meghan was ready to talk. Ready to hear him out. He cupped her face in his hands and shook his head. Trey looked tired, worn, the lines on his face were more prominent now. They had found an empty room on the first floor and locked themselves in. Meghan knew there were cameras in here, but she didn't care. The only person watching would be Damián and she trusted him. Completely. She had pulled down the blinds so the room would be darker, more intimate. He had tried to kiss her again. She had pulled back. She wanted to know what made him leave, and why he came back.

"You know why I came back, Meg. For you." Trey let go of her and shuffled backwards on the bed.

"Is there someone else Trey? I need to know the truth."

He looked away and then back again, noticed the startling blue of her eyes. He could not hold back anymore.

"My mother," he said simply.

Meghan knew Trey had been adopted. She had heard all the stories of his childhood from his adoptive mother, Rose, and she remembered how he had broken down one evening in front of them both, begging to know who his real mother was. Rose had begun to cry hysterically, and Trey had walked away with Meghan left to comfort the poor woman. This had been years ago, though; he had not brought it up again.

"Why didn't you come to me? I could have helped." Meghan reached for his hands, but he stood and walked away from her.

"Because I needed to do it on my own. I found out who she is, and I didn't think you'd want to be with me anymore." He started to weep now; his beautiful eyes filled with tears.

"I want to be with you, no matter what! I love you, Trey. I would never, ever leave you…"

"Unlike me," he mumbled.

"You did what you needed to do...Did you find what you were looking for?"

Trey shook his head and reached into his jacket, drawing out a crumpled piece of paper.

"Here," he whispered, "this is what she said."

Meghan took it and slowly pressed down the creases, smoothing the paper respectfully. She began to read. Trey watched her expression change.

"The...the lake house? How did she know?"

"She wasn't even there...she..." Trey's phone buzzed. He sniffed back the tears and looked at the screen. It was an unknown number, but he was intrigued. He answered and pressed the speakerphone.

"Yes?"

"Is this Trey Maguire?" asked a female voice.

"It is. Can I ask who's calling?" he swallowed down the lump in his throat.

Game Over

Viezmann bit into his ham sandwich. The computer screen in front of him detailed the findings from the Landley crash. So, the brakes had been tampered with, eh? He brushed the crumbs from the pathologist's report on his desk and grabbed it in both hands. He needed to chat to Preston Hargreaves.

****

Jocelyn had not left her motel room in days. But it meant she had had time to think. The Police had phoned her, taking her through it all, underlining the details. She would need to identify the body. After all, Joce was the only family Jinger had left. She wanted to make things right with her sister. And the only way was to talk to Preston.

****

Dellah had checked her emails on and off for the last two hours. Still nothing from Emilia. Things had been getting harder for Mitchell, too. He had become distant and preferred to shut himself in the conference room to make his calls. She knew he was asking for help from anyone who would give it. The hotel was now home to a scandal; Jinger's name was all over the news, her face making headlines Mitchell could not control. Dellah worried about her husband, worried about their investment, worried about their marriage. She was no fool. She had dug deep into his past and pulled out some weeds. But those weeds had started to grow back.

She swiped her phone screen and refreshed it one more time. Surely Emmy knew something…one new message. She opened it quickly and scrolled down the screen.

'Dellah,

Thanks for getting in touch. I was surprised to hear from you but not surprised to see that name. I'll put it out to my contacts and start the hunt again.

Best,

Emmy'

Dellah sighed with a palpable relief and threw her phone on Mitchell's desk. Damián wouldn't be getting away with it this time.

****

Preston's phone had been ringing nonstop since the news about Jinger broke. Newspapers, chat shows, police. He could not take any more. He had done nothing wrong. He had loved her. Someone must be settling him up. He ran through names in his head but none of them would go this far, would they? Lonnie? Surely not. What did he have to gain except pain through spite? He had switched his TV off, preferring to sit in the silence of his apartment. Suddenly, a familiar tune began to play. At first, he thought it was in his head, a memory that brought him pure joy. But it was his phone, her picture flashing up on the screen.

"Joce. Where are you?"

****

Officer Logan was keeping an eye on things at the hotel. Preston had not appeared yet and the only new faces were the male concierge, an older woman and that TV star, Troy something. Logan wondered why he was hiding out here. What scandal had brought him to The Beverly? He had managed to find a parking spot a short distance from the main entrance and decided to stay put for now. Viezmann had been in touch about the brakes. From now on, he decided, whatever the detective guessed was going to be true, even the suspicion that there was more to this than the jealousy of a spoiled brat rich boy. His radio kept interrupting his thoughts. And then he saw her, heading towards The Beverly. That same face but different hair. She seemed in a hurry. He watched her rush inside and decided to follow.

Together Again, Naturally

He stood alone in the darkness. His next move needed to be a good one.

****

Robyn had a huge smile on her face when she ended the call. Finally, something positive had happened. Something that was going to change her life for the better and no longer the worse.

****

Mitchell knew he was hiding from it all. It was all getting a little too much to manage. Maybe buying a place like The Beverly had been a mistake. Maybe buying a place like The Beverly had been the worst mistake he had ever made. He gathered his paperwork together and shoved it into his briefcase taking a fleeting look at the conference room. Never again, he thought and chuckled lightly. I'll find Dell and sort something out. He walked slowly to the door, closing it reverently behind him and moving down the corridor. A figure stood there. Waiting for him it seemed. A woman with the face of an angel.

****

Lonnie had decided to follow Robyn to the hotel. He had gulped down a couple of pints of water and called a taxi. Ending up in a ditch like Jinger was not on his priority list. He was going to tell her how bad it was and hope she would forgive him one last time. Because this was the last time. He did not want to do it anymore. It was not just hurting his bank account; it was killing his marriage.

The taxi turned around in the entrance to The Beverly, and he clambered out, passing a scruffy note to the driver.

"Watch yourself in there, mate," the man said, "not too safe right now."

"Thanks for the tip," Lonnie replied and headed inside.

The lobby was light and airy but as silent as a monastery. He was sure it was not meant to be. Two security guards seemed to be sleeping in the chairs by the door, their heads lolling. How useful, Lonnie thought, wondering where to go first. The main desk was empty. A computer screen was on; he could just see the images on it, presumably from internal and external cameras. He knew if he tried to ring her again, she would not answer so he went behind the desk and perused the screen.

"Can I help you?" called a female voice.

Lonnie looked up and noticed a name badge.

"I'm looking for my wife, actually. Perhaps you know where she is, Meghan?" His voice had lost its previous drunken slur but now sounded tired and worn down, husky and dry.

Meghan indicated that he should remove himself from her desk by stepping back and motioning with her outstretched arms. Lonnie conceded and made his way towards her, palms upwards.

"Who is your wife, Sir?"

"Robyn Latymer. Her brother, Preston, is a permanent resident here. You have at least heard of him?" OK, a bit unnecessary, but he needed to find Robyn before he chickened out.

The lift came to life and both Meghan and Lonnie turned.

Preston Hargreaves stepped out with a woman on each arm; his sister and his girlfriend, two complete opposites yet they held onto him, their one constant. Then followed another younger man, his arms reaching for Meghan.

Officer Logan strolled in and smirked.

"About time you showed up."

The voice did not belong to Logan. The voice came from beyond the foyer, beyond the now assembled group.

Damián.

****

Mitchell stared across his desk at the woman he thought was dead. That was the truth he had been told. She had not coped being locked away, so she took her own life instead. She had the same golden sparkle in those deep bronze eyes, the same wrinkle above her nose, the same strong lips he had kissed so passionately. It was hard to find any words. How can someone speak when they are looking into the eyes of the dead.

Melissa breathed in slowly and then placed her hand on her heart with the exhale. He had aged so beautifully, just as she knew he would.

****

Dellah sat facing the detective, trying hard not to fidget. Her right foot kept drumming against the floor, and she had to push down on her leg to soothe the anguish.

"He's still at the Hotel." she reiterated. Her rush to get to Viezmann had meant she'd had to leave Randy at his friend's house for the night; the kid's mother wasn't exactly on board with the arrangement but Dellah's ability at persuasion was unmatched.

The Detective was looking at her very closely. He already knew Preston was not a suspect. The guy just was not savvy enough. It just did not make sense. But this new name was not so new to Viezmann. He had heard it and many like it before.

"I got your email. It's been a long time since I've seen the name 'Dellah Ramsey' in print." Viezmann smiled wistfully.

"Officer Logan is on duty there. Let's shut it down." He paused and looked straight into her eyes.

"You are very brave Miss Ramsay. You were one of the best journalists I worked with." He reached out and they shook hands, like old friends.

How sweet it is...

From the outside, The Beverly looks imposing. Its structure is not dissimilar to regular resort hotels, yet it pulls itself back from the road, back from the tourists, back from the regular lives that exist around it. Locals tend to avoid walking near it. They skirt around its edges as if fearing the secrets it holds. The previous owner, Carlton Hargreaves was not known for his amiability. In fact, he preferred to live in the hotel himself and was seldom seen beyond its doors. However, Mitchell Hudson was seen and was known to the community. He donated to local causes, appeared as often as he could and smiled that award-winning smile of his. Yet still, The Beverly was not open to those without the means to stay there. Visitors would enjoy trying to celebrity-spot from the comfort of their cars. No-one would dare go through that enticingly decadent front door.

****

Preston gripped Jocelyn's arm. Robyn stood boldly in front of them. Lonnie was rooted to the tiles. Trey held onto Meghan, but Meghan loosened his grip. She looked at Damián, the friend she thought she knew and felt suddenly lost. He held something slick in his left hand and his right twitched unconsciously.

He had decided not to leave without fighting first. Plans did not always work out. His past had taught him that.

Logan checked his watch, felt his phone vibrate in his pocket and slid his hand onto his gun.

****

Mitchell and Melissa still sat in his office but now they had broken the silence. Words had begun to tumble out of Mitchell like an avalanche. Truths were being shared. Realities understood. New information brought to light.

So, Mitchell had a son. Another son.

And that was why she faked her death. She could not raise a child in prison, his child. He was young, too young to be a father. She needed to hide it all and so she died, just for a while. And, when her daughter needed her, she came back. Her sentence was overturned, thanks to a generous benefactor high in the political and legal ranks. She had literally gotten away with murder.

Mitchell did not know how to feel. Then they heard the shouts.

****

Sirens. Lights. Stretchers. Comforting arms and warm jackets. The Beverly is lit from above. Helicopters circle, rotators whir.

An ambulance starts up. A body is bundled inside, and the doors slam shut.

The Hudsons watch from the back of their limo as it speeds off down the lane; turning their heads away from what was once a perfect dream but became a perfect nightmare.

Lonnie clutches his wife's hand as a paramedic checks her then grabs his brother-in-law in an embrace.

Carlos and Candice surround Jocelyn and Meghan, pressing down on wounds and wiping away tears.

Melissa holds Trey as close as she can and feels his heart beating next to hers…

And the cameras arrive again to take a snapshot of the lives and loves no longer hidden behind The Beverly's exclusive walls.

Coming soon...
The second book in *The Beverly* series

Relationships are tested, more truths revealed, and a familiar face makes a comeback...

Printed in Great Britain
by Amazon